STANDARD LOAN

Merthyr Tydfil Learning Resources Centre
Tel: (01685) 726005

Books are to be returned on or before the last date below

Merthyr Tydfil Learning Resources Centre CF48 1AR
University of Glamorgan

21st Century Skills Library

HEALTHY FOR LIFE

MOUNTAIN BIKING

Michael Teitelbaum

Cherry Lake Publishing
Ann Arbor, Michigan

Published in the United States of America by Cherry Lake Publishing
Ann Arbor, MI
www.cherrylakepublishing.com

Content Adviser: Thomas Sawyer, EdD, Professor of Recreation and Sports Management,
Indiana State University, Terre Haute, Indiana

Photo Credits: Page 7, © Bettmann/Corbis; page 18, © Tim Kiusalaas/Corbis; page 28,
© Tim de Waele/Corbis

Library of Congress Cataloging-in-Publication Data
Teitelbaum, Michael.
  Mountain biking / by Michael Teitelbaum.
    p. cm. — (Healthy for life)
  Includes index.
  ISBN-13: 978-1-60279-016-2 (lib. bdg.)   978-1-60279-087-2 (paperback)
  ISBN-10: 1-60279-016-7 (lib. bdg.)   1-60279-087-6 (paperback)
  1. All terrain cycling—Juvenile literature. I. Title. II. Series.
  GV1056.T45 2008
  796.63—dc22   2007007730

Cherry Lake Publishing would like to acknowledge the work of
The Partnership for 21st Century Skills.
Please visit www.21stcenturyskills.org for more information.

TABLE OF CONTENTS

CHAPTER ONE

THE RIDE OF YOUR LIFE!

Are you ready for a real thrill? Try mountain biking!

You're flying down a mountain trail, bouncing over rocks, jumping over logs, racing the wind. You're on a mountain bike, having the time of your life. You've probably ridden a bike of some kind—in a playground, on a quiet street, or even on a smooth, paved trail. But when you hop on a mountain bike, you're entering a whole new world of fun and fitness. The sport of mountain biking combines the thrill of riding a bike with the beauty of exploring nature's wonders. On a mountain bike, you'll discover wooded trails and rugged mountain paths as you pedal.

If you enjoy hiking and you enjoy bike riding, mountain biking is the perfect way to combine the two. You can cover much more ground in a single day of outdoor fun than walking, so you get to see more of the great outdoors.

You can't just use a regular bike to go off-road like this, though. Mountain bikes are specially made to stand up to the punishment of dirt trails, ruts, rock, or logs—all the while giving you a comfortable, safe ride.

If you know how to ride a bike, you already know how to ride a mountain bike. Anyone can do it—even if you don't live near a mountain. Mountain bikes are great for riding on dirt roads or on hiking or horseback

If you think mountain biking is as easy as riding down to the corner on your paved street, think again! Mountain biking can be challenging, but it can make you feel great. Mountain biking requires you to push yourself beyond your basic skills as a rider, and it improves your athletic ability and stamina. Once you make the commitment and take the initiative to start training—with steady work, self-direction, and self-motivation—you will surpass your goals as a biker.

riding trails. Many local and state parks allow mountain biking on their trails. And if you live near a ski area, many of them allow people to use their slopes for mountain biking during the off-season.

Mountain biking is fairly easy. By using the correct equipment and understanding what you need to stay safe and healthy, this can be a sport you enjoy throughout your life.

So how did it all start? Bicycles have been around since the early 1800s. Mountain biking started in the late 1890s. The U.S. Army decided to test these rugged versions of their slimmer, lighter cousins to transport soldiers across the harsh **terrain** of the western United States. A group of soldiers rode mountain bikes from Missoula, Montana, past Yellowstone Park and over the Rocky Mountains, to St. Louis, Missouri, a total of 1,900 miles (3,000 kilometers). These first mountain bikes weighed about 90 pounds (40 kilograms)—compare that to today's mountain bikes, which weigh about 25 pounds (10 kg). These bikes passed this grueling test (as did the soldiers), but the army decided to focus on motorized forms of transportation instead, and the bikes were put aside.

Modern mountain biking began in the 1950s when a bike rider named John Finley Scott took a standard bike and added fat balloon tires, a straight **handlebar**, extra **gears**, and more powerful brakes. Scott rode his homemade creation on mountain trails in Oregon and California.

A bicycling craze swept the country in the late 19th century. By the 1890s, there were 10 million bikes in the United States.

Mountain biking began to grow in popularity in the mid-1970s when Gary Fisher of California began building, riding, and selling old beach bikes that he modified with balloon tires and extra-strong brakes. Lots of people bought and rode these bikes, which they called clunkers. A company called Specialized Bicycle Components made the first mass-produced mountain

Learning & Innovation Skills

The U.S. Army's inventive use of mountain bikes helped the sport of mountain biking gain popularity. People saw how the development and implementation of a new kind of bicycle made soldiers more mobile and able to travel longer distances in shorter amounts of time compared to walking or hiking. While the army didn't continue using bikes, the creativity that was applied to biking inspired an entirely new perspective on what bicycles could do.

bikes in the early 1980s. Their original model was called the Stumpjumper.

Now that you know a little bit about the history of mountain biking, here are some terms you can use that will make you sound like an old pro:

1) **Knobbies:** Wide, fat tires used on mountain bikes (wider than on standard bikes), with raised rubber bumps and deep tread.

2) **Derailleur:** A mechanism that moves the bike's chain from one sprocket wheel to another when the rider shifts gears. Mountain bikes have a front derailleur and a back derailleur.

3) **Cranks:** Pieces of metal that connect the chain to the pedals to help turn the bike's wheels.

4) **Feathering:** To gently squeeze and release the brakes over and over, to safely control the bike's speed.

5) **Fishtail:** When the back tire of a mountain bike slides quickly to the side. This usually happens when the rider brakes suddenly and squeezes the brakes too hard.

6) **Hop:** To lift the front wheel of your bike off the ground, using the handlebars, in order to go over an obstacle in your path.

7) **Toe clips:** Small cagelike pieces of metal into which a rider slips his or her feet in order to hold the feet onto the pedal.

8) **Baby heads:** Small rocks on a trail that are about the size of a baby's head.

9) **Bagging a peak**: Making it to the top of a mountain.

10) **Biff**: To crash.

Now that you've got the lingo down, let's talk about getting the right equipment to ensure that your ride is fun and safe!

A mountain biker races down a hillside.

CHAPTER TWO

WHAT YOU NEED: EQUIPMENT AND TRAINING

Mountain bikes have thick tires and sturdy frames.

It all begins with the mountain bike. It's your galloping steed, your faithful companion, not to mention your wicked cool ride! A good bike that you are comfortable with makes all the difference between a day of fun and adventure, and a miserable, bone-rattling, frustrating experience.

Mountain bikes differ from regular street bikes in many important ways. They have stronger, sturdier **frames** to stand up to the bumps and bounces on uneven, rocky riding surfaces. The tires are much wider and have deeper **tread** and rubber bumps to give you better **traction** on dirt. They have many more gears (up to 21, instead of the usual 10 on a standard bike) to make it easier to pedal going up steep hills. The handlebars on a mountain bike are made of one straight piece of metal. They're not curved like on standard bikes. This design helps to give the rider greater control.

Many mountain bikes have **suspension** systems, such as springs, to absorb the jolts of a rough trail and smooth out your ride. Mountain bikes with suspension systems cost more, but the reward is a much more comfortable ride.

Mountain bikes use gears and chains to turn the wheels and make you go. The **brake levers** are on the handlebars. When the levers are squeezed, the **brake pads** on either side of the front and back wheels close, slowing the bike down.

The pedals are what you use to apply power to the bike. Most mountain bikes come with toe clips that hold your feet onto the pedals, yet allow them to slip out easily if you need to.

Choosing the right size bike is important for both your enjoyment and your safety. One simple way to do this is to straddle the bike, feet flat on the ground. You should have between 2 and 4 inches (5 and 10 centimeters) of room between you and the bar. If so, you've picked the right size.

As with any bike riding, a helmet is a must for mountain biking. Bike helmets are made of lightweight hard foam or plastic and should be well **ventilated**. Your chances of running into unexpected obstacles or difficult terrain are great when biking on trails or through the woods, which means your chances of falling are greater than while biking on a smooth road.

Helmets, kneepads, and padded gloves help protect mountain bikers from injury.

Wear your helmet whenever you're on your bike. It's as simple as that.

Padded gloves help absorb the bumps and make gripping the handlebars easier. They also keep you from getting blisters and will offer some protection to your hands when you fall.

Protective glasses or goggles serve a number of purposes. They keep branches from poking you in the eyes while riding on a narrow path in the woods. They also keep flying material such as dust, dirt, pebbles, twigs, and bugs (yes, bugs!) from getting into your eyes. And they prevent the wind from making your eyes tear up.

Padded bike shorts will make a long, bumpy ride much more comfortable. The rest of your riding outfit depends on the weather. Remember, the difference in temperature between the top and base of a mountain can be great, so if you're riding up and down a mountain, dress in layers. You don't want to be caught with too much or not enough clothing. And choose clothing (especially the

21st Century Content

The only two essential pieces of equipment you'll really need to go mountain biking are the bike and the helmet. Everything else will just add to the enjoyment of your ride. It's important, however, to make appropriate economic choices when purchasing your equipment. Here's what you can expect to pay, so make sure to save properly:

1) Mountain bikes: $70–$2,000
2) Helmets: $35–$150
3) Gloves: $20–$40
4) Goggles: $30–$100
5) Riding shorts: $40–$90

When you mountain bike, you encounter many different terrains and conditions. Both you and your bike have to be flexible and adaptable to deal with whatever challenges you face. A bike's gears give it flexibility. The gears allow you to keep pedaling in a smooth, steady motion as the slope and terrain of the trail change. In lower gears, the pedals move more easily. So if you need to climb a hill, you can do it with less effort. If you need power and speed on flat ground, higher gears deliver greater power with each spin of the pedals, but these gears require more effort on your part. As you become a more experienced rider, you'll glide from one gear to another, shifting up or down, to keep yourself pedaling and on the move.

bottom layer closest to your body) made of polyester fabrics that wick (carry) sweat away from your body.

Drink lots of water before you set out, and bring lots of water with you, to keep yourself **hydrated**. Continue drinking water after you are done, too. Bring along snacks such as energy bars, to make sure you get enough calories. You'll burn a lot of calories on a long ride, and you're not likely to find a convenience store in the middle of the woods to grab a snack.

To succeed at mountain biking, you need **endurance**, strength, and riding skill. The first two come from exercise. The skill comes from practice. Start with short, easy rides—not too long, not too steep, not too rough. Slowly build up to longer, more challenging rides, so mountain biking remains a fun adventure and you never feel out of control.

CHAPTER THREE

STAYING SAFE ON YOUR BIKE

Almost all mountain bikers crash at one point or another, but if they're wearing good safety gear, they're less likely to be hurt.

The single most important piece of safety equipment for mountain biking is your helmet. If you ride a mountain bike, chances are you are going fall sometimes. So it's essential to protect your head. Get a helmet that fits, and adjust it properly. The rest of mountain bike safety relies on using common sense and having a basic knowledge of what you're likely to encounter out on the trail.

Rocks, logs, and other things that go bump will be a constant companion on your ride. The best way to handle these obstacles safely is by shifting your weight back and pulling up on your handlebars, lifting your front tire up and over the obstacle. Once your front tire has returned to the ground, lean forward to reduce the weight on your back tire as it passes over the **obstruction**.

Try your best not to ride through mud on a path. It's slippery for you, does great damage to the path, and causes soil **erosion**, ruining the path for others. (Read about your responsibilities in Chapter Four.) If you don't have enough room to safely ride around the mud, get off your bike and walk it around—so that your weight is not on the bike, which presses it into the ground. The same thing goes for hills that are too steep to ride up and trail surfaces that are too broken up to ride on safely. Get off and walk the bike.

The safest way to walk your bike is by placing one hand on the back of the seat and the other hand

To go up steep, rough hills, you have to get off your bike and push.

on the handlebars. This allows you to lean on your bike for support as you roll it up a steep hill.

Don't ride through water such as a river or a stream. It's very slippery, and you could fall onto the wet rocks. Get off your bike and carry it across. The best way to carry your bike is to grab it by the middle of the bar and lift it onto your shoulder. Let your shoulder

21st Century Content

What kinds of supplies should you pack when you go mountain biking? When you head out on the trail, you should bring extra water, healthy snacks, a basic first aid kit with bandages and antibacterial cream, sunscreen, insect repellent, extra clothing, sunglasses, rain gear, and your cell phone, if you have one, just in case. Bringing along a map of the area you'll be biking in and a compass is also a good idea, in case you lose your way. These precautions are necessary. Taking them demonstrates that you are responsible and understand the preventive measures you can and should take on the trail.

Riding through streams is dangerous. Carry your bike instead.

support the weight as you grip the handlebars with your other hand to guide and steady the bike.

Holes, ruts, and ditches also pose safety hazards. Small holes and ruts should be avoided if at all possible. If you need to ride across a large ditch, lean your weight back as you start to go down into the ditch. At the bottom, lean forward and crouch low to give yourself better traction. And then, as you head up the other side of the ditch, straighten up and bend your elbows to take some weight off of your front tire.

Be careful when riding on small rocks or loose gravel. These can be slippery. If you must ride on these surfaces, keep your weight back to give yourself better traction. If you need to make a turn on gravel, you can help support your weight and keep yourself from falling by dragging your foot on the ground. Use your right foot for right turns and your left foot for left turns.

Now that you know how to stay safe, it's time to make sure that other riders and the beautiful places you ride in stay safe as well.

21st Century Content

Before you head out to the trail, you should know how to handle any injuries that might occur. Always have your first aid kit and a cell phone with you. Talk to your doctor about the best way to treat common injuries. These include abrasions, cuts, puncture wounds, fractures, sprains, strains, heat emergencies (heat exhaustion, heat cramps, and heat stroke), bee stings, and blisters.

CHAPTER FOUR

BEING A GOOD GUEST: BIKING RESPONSIBLY

The thrill of mountain biking comes from the fun and challenge of the ride. But as you are out there enjoying the beautiful outdoors, remember you have a responsibility. It's your job to do your best to leave the park, trail, or mountain where you are riding exactly the way you found it. The most obvious rule is don't litter! *If you carry it in, carry it out!* Wrappers

Being out in the beautiful countryside is one of the great pleasures of mountain biking.

from snacks and empty water bottles should be placed into trashcans or taken with you.

The International Mountain Bicycling Association (IMBA), the main mountain biking organization, has established a set of rules for being a good guest while mountain biking. Most require nothing more than common sense.

Help keep trails clean by picking up litter and putting it in trash cans.

Global awareness extends to every part of your life, including the natural surroundings of mountain bike trails. Caring for the environment will ensure that you and others will enjoy the beauty of the diverse plants and animals along your favorite trails for years to come. In addition to taking care of your own garbage, if you see garbage and litter on the trail, pick it up and throw it out.

Learning & Innovation Skills

Safety cannot be the responsibility of one person. Everyone has to follow the rules and do their part to keep the trails fun and safe. This requires developing good on-trail communication skills. With these skills, you will be able to collaborate with other bikers to make sure that all signs, warnings, and rules on the bike path are followed.

Never bike on a closed trail.

Only ride your bike on open trails on which bikes are allowed. If a trail is closed, it's closed for a good reason, so don't take that trail. Always respect private property. Never trespass.

Leave no trace. In addition to not littering, this rule includes not intentionally **skidding** your tires. This action damages trails, causes erosion, and ruins the surface for everyone.

Always remain in control of your bike. Don't speed or try wild stunts. This is dangerous to you and to other riders.

Be considerate of other bikers, hikers, or horseback riders who are sharing the trail with you. Slow down when you see other people, and signal so that they are aware of your presence. A friendly greeting or bicycle bell will do the trick. Always give the right-of-way to people on horses and to those bikers riding uphill (since riding downhill is a much easier task!).

If you come upon an animal, slow down and pass at a safe distance. Never try to scare the animal, and never make a loud noise. Frightening animals is not just rude; it's also dangerous. Besides, you are in their home. Show some respect.

A little respect for others and for the environment, and some common sense will go a long way to a safe, enjoyable day of riding.

Learning & Innovation Skills

Are you interested in meeting other people who like mountain biking? The International Mountain Bicycling Association (IMBA), formed in 1988, is a nonprofit educational organization whose mission is to create and preserve trails for mountain bikers around the world. Environmental responsibility is its main concern. The IMBA encourages low-impact riding (which doesn't damage trails) and helps maintain trails. As a volunteer, you can collaborate with other bikers to make sure trails are preserved for future use. The IMBA is made up of more than 450 local mountain biking clubs and has 32,000 members in all 50 U.S. states, most Canadian provinces, and 30 other countries.

CHAPTER FIVE

THE ADDED BONUS: HEALTH BENEFITS OF MOUNTAIN BIKING

Mountain biking is great for your health. It builds up muscles, helps to strengthen your heart, and burns calories. It also sharpens your sense of balance and your reflexes.

Mountain biking is good for the body and the mind.

*Before you head for the hills, build up your strength
and endurance by biking on flat roads.*

The two key elements in training for mountain biking are endurance
and strength. Aerobic training such as walking, running, and, of course,
biking itself helps you build up the endurance you need for long days of
mountain biking. It also has the health benefit of relieving stress, helping

It takes strong muscles to bike up a mountain.

you lose weight, and making your heart healthier. The best way to build up your endurance is to start riding on a flat paved road. Ride for 30 minutes the first day, then increase to 45 minutes the next, then an hour, and so on. When you can ride for a number of hours without getting winded, you're ready to take on the hills and trails of mountain biking.

Strength training with weights builds up your muscles, and strong muscles help you ride more easily. Your leg muscles are the most important muscles for mountain biking. Building up your muscles also helps prevent injuries. With strong leg muscles, you will have no trouble reaching the top of the mountain.

You can use either free weights or weight machines for strength training. Before beginning a

21st Century Content

Compare the approximate number of calories a 100-pound (45-kilogram) person burns in one hour of mountain biking to the number burned in one hour of other activities. If you weigh less, you'll burn fewer calories in the same amount of time. If you weigh more, you'll burn more calories in the same amount of time.

Mountain biking: 502
Rock climbing: 498
Playing basketball: 498
Cross-country skiing: 472
Running: 456
Downhill skiing: 396
Backpacking: 318
Swimming: 276
Bowling: 138
Playing Frisbee: 138
Brushing your teeth: 114
Talking on the phone: 48
Watching TV or playing video games: 48

strength training routine, talk to your doctor to make sure your body can handle the stress. Once you get the okay, find a coach or trainer who works with teens and can create a routine that's best for you.

Both men and women compete in cross-country cycling events at the Olympics.

As with any sport, warming up before you ride and cooling down and stretching after you ride are very important. To warm up and cool down, take a slow, easy ride on a flat area or walk around for a little while. When you stretch, hold each stretch for 30 seconds. This loosens up the muscles, making it less likely you'll strain or pull them during your next ride.

Did you know that mountain biking is an Olympic sport? It made its debut at the 1996 Olympic Games in Atlanta, Georgia. As part of the Olympics, mountain biking is officially called cross-country cycling, and both men and women compete in the sport.

Mountain biking is also featured in the X Games, the top competitive event in the world of extreme sports. Riders from around the world compete in a series of mountain biking events, including snow racing, in which riders speed down snowy ski slopes at 70 miles (110 kilometers) per hour!

Stay fit, learn and practice the skills of riding, train, warm up, cool down, stretch afterward, and get the right equipment—and soon you'll be racing down a mountain or pedaling slowly through a gorgeous wilderness.

GLOSSARY

brake levers (BRAYK LEV-urz) the control devices that you press to make the brakes work, usually located on the handlebars

brake pads (BRAYK PADZ) the parts attached to the wheels that close on the wheel rims when the brake lever is squeezed to slow the bike down

endurance (en-DUR-enss) the ability to maintain an activity for a long period of time

erosion (ih-ROH-zhuhn) the wearing away of soil

frames (FRAYMZ) the structures of bikes, made up of metal tubing

gears (GEEHRZ) mechanisms that change how easy or hard it is to pedal

handlebar (HAN-duhl-bar) the metal bar at the front of the bike used for steering

hydrated (HYE-drayt-ed) having enough water

obstruction (uhb-STRUHKT-shun) something blocking your path

skidding (SKIH-ding) dragging your tires across a riding surface in a quick, lurching manner

suspension (suh-SPEN-shun) the part of a bike that absorbs bumps to create a smoother ride for you

terrain (tuh-RAYN) the surface of the ground on which you ride

traction (TRAK-shun) the ability to grip the ground to keep your tires from slipping

tread (TRED) the grooves in a tire that help it grip the ground better

ventilated (VEN-tuh-late-ed) open so that hot air can escape

For More Information

Books

MacAulay, Kelley, and Bobbie Kalman. *Extreme Mountain Biking.*
New York: Crabtree Publishing Company, 2006.

Osborne, Ian. *Mountain Biking* (Extreme Sports). Minneapolis: Lerner Sports, 2003.

Wurdinger, Scott, and Leslie Rapparlie. *Mountain Biking* (Adventure
Sports). Mankato, MN: Creative Education, 2007.

Web Sites

GORP: Biking
gorp.away.com/gorp/activity/biking.htm
A helpful listing of trails, events, clubs, and more

International Mountain Bicycling Association
www.imba.com
The organization's official Web site

Mountain Bike
www.bicycling.com/channel/0,6609,s1-6-0-0-0,00.html
A good general information site about the sport

INDEX

ABOUT THE AUTHOR

Michael Teitelbaum has been a writer and editor of children's books and magazines for more than twenty years. He was editor of *Little League Magazine for Kids;* is the author of a two-volume encyclopedia on the Baseball Hall of Fame, published by Grolier; and was the writer/project editor of *Breaking Barriers: In Sports, In Life,* a character education program based on the life of Jackie Robinson, created for Scholastic Inc. and Major League Baseball. Michael is the author of *Great Moments in Women's Sports,* published by Gareth Stevens, and *Sports in America: The 1980s,* published by Facts on File. His latest work of fiction is *The Scary States of America,* published by Delacorte in 2007. Michael and his wife, Sheleigah, live in New York City, where they root for the Mets.